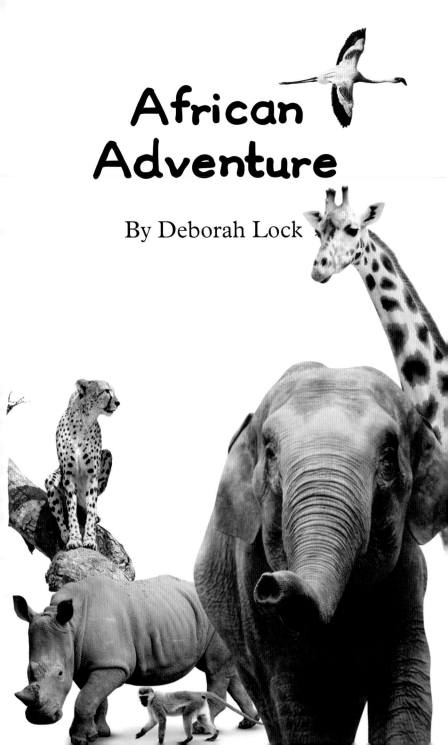

African Adventure

By Deborah Lock

LONDON, NEW YORK, MUNICH,
MELBOURNE, AND DELHI

DK LONDON

Series Editor Deborah Lock
Project Art Editor Hoa Luc
Production Editor Francesca Wardell

Reading Consultant Shirley Bickler

DK DELHI

Editor Nandini Gupta
Designer Shruti Soharia Singh
DTP Designer Anita Yadav
Picture Researcher Sumedha Chopra
Dy. Managing Editor Soma B. Chowdhury
Design Consultant Shefali Upadhyay

First published in Great Britain by
Dorling Kindersley Limited
80 Strand, London, WC2R 0RL

Copyright © 2014 Dorling Kindersley Limited
A Penguin Company

10 9 8 7 6 5 4 3 2 1
001—195864—January/2014

A CIP catalogue record for this book is available from the British Library.

ISBN: 978-1-40934-725-5

Printed and bound in China by South China Printing Company.

The publisher would like to thank the following for their kind permission
to reproduce their photographs:
(Key: a-above; b-below/bottom; c-centre; f-far; l-left; r-right; t-top)
1 Dreamstime.com: Dragoneye (cra), Fotolia: Adrio (cl); Proma (tr). 4 Getty Images: Nigel Pavitt
/ AWL Images (b). 5 Dreamstime.com: Aughty Venable (t). 10-11 Dreamstime.com: Alextara
(background). 11 Corbis: Katie Garrod / Jai (br). 15 Alamy Images: Richard Garvey-Williams (t),
Corbis: Barry Lewis / In Pictures (b). 23 Dorling Kindersley: Rough Guides.
25 Getty Images: Sune Wendelboe / Lonely Planet Images (t). 28 Fotolia: AGfoto (cl, bc).
34 Dreamstime.com: Lian Deng (bl); Stu Porter (br). 38 Dreamstime.com: Yew Wah Kok (ca).
41 Dreamstime.com: Richard Carey (t). 42 Corbis: Jami Tarris (t), Dreamstime.com: Martesia
Bezuidenhout (b). 44-45 Corbis: Joe McDonald (t). 44 Corbis: ZSSD / Minden Pictures (bl).
Dorling Kindersley: Rough Guides (ca). Dreamstime.com: Stefanie Van Der Vinden (cla).
45 Dreamstime.com: Duncan Noakes (c). 46 Corbis: Gallo Images (b). 47 Getty Images: AFP (t).
49 Dreamstime.com: Hedrus (b). 52 Dreamstime.com: Sandra Van Der Steen.
54 Corbis: Jake Warga (bl). 55 Corbis: Dlillc (bl); Antony Njuguna / X90056 / Reuters (tc).
56 Dreamstime.com: Daleen Loest (cb). 57 Corbis: Martin Harvey (t). 58 Dorling Kindersley:
Jerry Young (bc). 58-59 Corbis: Aditya Singh / imagebroker (Background).
59 Corbis: Dlillc (bc); Nigel Pavitt / Jai (bl); Nigel J. Dennis / Gallo Images (br)
Jacket images: Back cover © Herbert Kehrer / Imagebroker / Corbis
All others © Dorling Kindersley

All other images © Dorling Kindersley

For further information see: www.dkimages.com

Discover more at
www.dk.com

Contents

My Safari Diary by Katie Collins

I am now settled into camp. We have been travelling for two days. The best part of our long flight was flying over the snow-capped Mount Kenya. After landing in Nairobi, we had a three-hour bumpy jeep trip.

Mount Kenya

We have already seen some large birds. There were marabou storks on the edge of the towns.
They are ugly!

I am very excited about this week. I wonder if I will get to see all of the Big Five: the lion, African elephant, Cape buffalo, leopard and rhinoceros.

Day 1

6.00 a.m. Breakfast

6.30 a.m. Game drive

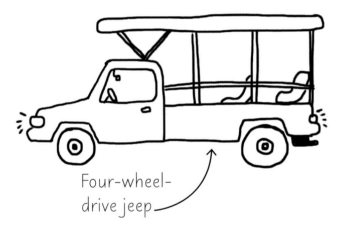

Four-wheel-
drive jeep

12.00 noon Lunch

1.30 p.m. River trip

7.00 p.m. Dinner and
campfire stories

I have just had a quick rest.
Our morning game drive was
worth the early start though.
There were many animals
roaming the savannah before
the heat of the day.

Gazelles and the small dik-diks grazed among the herds of zebras and wildebeest. There are millions of zebras and wildebeest in this area at this time of year. They will stay a month or two to eat before migrating on.

Zebras and wildebeest on the move. Watch out behind you!

We watched a cheetah. She had killed an impala. She let her cubs feed first. Giraffes strutted proudly, stopping to nibble at the thornbushes. It is amazing how close we can get to these animals in our jeep.

Do you know what migrating means? If not, look in the glossary!

African Antelopes

Here's a spotters' guide to identifying some of the many types of antelope found in the savannah.

1. Gerenuk

Spot by its long neck and long legs. The male has thick, ringed horns.

2. Topi

Spot this medium–size antelope by the dark patches on its face and its upper legs.

3. Thomson's gazelle

Look out for the black stripes on its face and sides.

4. Dik-dik

A small antelope that has large dark marks within a white ring around its eyes.

5. Greater kudu

Look out for the white stripes on its body and the line of white between its eyes. The male has long spiral horns.

6. Gemsbok

Males and females have long, spear-like horns. Also look out for the black-and-white markings on their faces and legs.

We spent the afternoon on the river.
We saw crocodiles basking in
the sun on the muddy riverbanks.
Their mouths were open.
They looked scary.

We came across a few hippo pods,
too. Hippos are huge but most of
the time you can only see the top
of their heads. They peer over the
water plants. Each time, our guide
slowed the boat and kept a safe
distance away. He knew the danger.
Hippos have been known to tip
over boats.

Our guide pointed out and named the water-birds. He even spotted a green snake hiding in a tree that overhung the river. He took us close so that we could see its skin. Luckily, this was not the venomous green mamba, but a much smaller harmless snake.

We had a magical evening. We sat outside around a roaring campfire. The stars sparkled above us. A tribesman told some mythical stories from all over Africa.

The World Tree

In the beginning, people and animals were created and lived together peacefully under the ground.

They all spoke the same language. One day, the Creator built a new world with a giant tree, spreading out over the land, and laden with good things in its branches.

He made a hole to bring the people and animals up to this new world.

They were amazed. The Creator warned them not to make fire.

As the sun set, the people and animals all gathered beneath the tree.

The people became colder and colder during the night.

They shivered and were worried.

The people panicked and made

a fire. As they sat in the glow and warmth of the flames, they turned happily to their friends, the animals. But the animals had fled, terrified of the fire.

"Come back!" the people cried, but the animals no longer understood them and ran further away. The special friendship between people and animals was broken.

Day 2

8.00 a.m. Breakfast

10.00 a.m. Waterhole watching

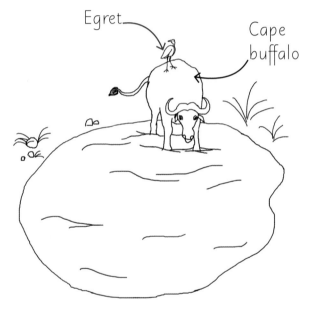

Egret

Cape buffalo

1.00 p.m. Lunch

3.30 p.m. Bush walk

7.00 p.m. Dinner and games

There is a waterhole in front of
our camp that we can see from
our tents. It has been busy with
animals visiting all morning.
I was very excited when a herd of
Cape buffalo came along to drink.
This is my first of the Big Five.

I used binoculars to take a closer look at the smaller birds. Some oxpeckers and cattle egrets perched on the backs of the buffalo. Every now and then, they pecked off a bug from the buffalo's skin. A busy weaver bird was collecting twigs. It wove them into its nest in a tree nearby.

Some cheeky vervet monkeys scampered along the wooden railings around our tent. We were told not to have food around. Now I know why! They were clever and fearless raiders. The troop was after anything they could find.

Before we set out on our afternoon bush walk, our guide gave a safety talk. He told us to stay close together and not to run.
We also had to be quiet if the guide signalled with his hands.

A Maasai guide led from the front and our nature guide walked at the back of our group. We had only just started when we came upon a troop of baboons.
They were relaxing on some rocks. Some of the younger ones were playing in the branches of the trees above them.

Find out more about the Maasai people on page 54.

Most of the time we walked through the open grass areas. The grazing animals were always alert. I could understand why! The longer grass was a perfect hiding place for hunting animals. Lions and cheetahs could watch and wait for the right moment to leap into action.

The guide showed us the tracks of animals in the mud. On our way back to the camp, we had to keep very still as the troop of baboons strolled past. They were setting out to find food.

What words would you use to describe the movement of a baboon?

Animal Tracks

Here's a spotters' guide to identifying some of the many types of footprints seen on the ground.

| Lion | Leopard | Cheetah |

| Elephant | Rhino | Hippo |

| Zebra | Aardvark | Hyena |

Dik-dik

Thomson's gazelle

Grant's gazelle

Impala

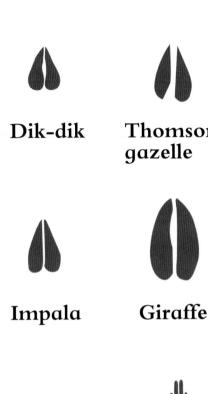

Giraffe

Water buffalo

Baboon

Colobus monkey

Porcupine

Mongoose

Vervet monkey

Honey badger

Mancala

This evening, we are being taught to play an African game called Mancala. It is an ancient game based on sowing seeds.

A game for 2 players

You will need:

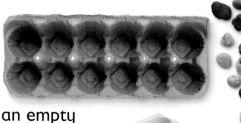

an empty
12-egg
carton

a yoghurt pot for
each player

48 small stones

How to set up

Place four stones in each of the 12 holes. Players face each other and place their pots on their right side of the carton.

How to play

1. A player picks up all of the stones in one of the holes on his/her side.

2. The player goes anti-clockwise, dropping a stone in each hole until they run out.

3. If the player passes his/her own pot, he/she drops one of the stones into it. If the other player's pot is passed, then miss it out.

4. The player gets a free turn if he/she drops the last stone into his/her pot.

5. If the last stone dropped is into an empty hole, the player takes all the stones in the hole opposite and puts them into his/her pot.

6. The game ends when all six holes on one side of the carton are empty.

How to score

The player with any remaining stones on his/her side of the carton adds these to his/her pot.

The winner is the player with the most stones in his/her pot.

Day 3

6.00 a.m. Breakfast

6.30 a.m. Radio tracking lions

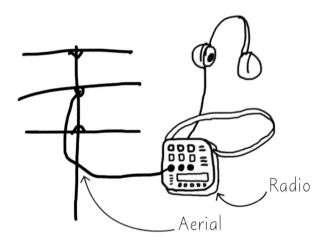

Radio

Aerial

12.00 noon Lunch

1.30 p.m. Visit Lake Nakuru

6.00 p.m. Preparing dinner

I have seen not just one lion but a
whole pride this morning! We went
out early with a research team who
monitor the lions in this area.
They have put a radio collar on
one of the females from each pride.
This helps the team find the prides.

The pride we followed this morning had three lionesses, eight cubs and one large lion. The team could identify each lion by their whisker-spot pattern. They had names for each one. We found the pride drinking by a small waterhole.

Whisker spots

The lionesses were thirsty after hunting during the night-time. The pride then found a cool place in the shade to rest. The cubs though were very playful.

The team took photos and collected lion scat (poop) and hairs. This was to help them collect information about the pride.

Here are some lion cubs' names:
Zuri [ZUH-ree] means "beautiful" in Swahili.
Baruti [ba-ROO-tee] is an African name meaning "teacher".
Nasieku is a Maasai name meaning "she who comes first".
What name would you give to a lion cub?

African Big Cats File

Leopard

Size: 70 cm (28 in.) tall
Weight: 60 kg (130 lb)
Top speed: 80 kph
(50 mph)
Noise: rasp
Vision: 6x better
than humans
Threat: endangered

Cheetah

Size: 75 cm (30 in.) tall
Weight: 65 kg (145 lb)
Top speed: 102 kph
(64 mph)
Noise: chirp, which
carries 2 km (1.2 mi)
Vision: 5 km (3 mi);
wider vision than humans
Threat: vulnerable

Male lion

Size: 90 cm (35 in.) tall
Weight: 180 kg (400 lb)
Top speed: 80 kph (50 mph)
Noise: roar, which carries 8 km (5 mi)
Vision: 5x better than humans
Threat: vulnerable

Serval

Size: 55 cm (22 in.) tall
Weight: 20 kg (45 lb)
Top speed: 80 kph (50 mph)
Noise: cry and grumble
Threat: endangered

This afternoon, we drove to Lake Nakuru. The shoreline was a mass of pink. As we drove closer, we could make out thousands of flamingos. They were dipping their beaks to feed on the algae (water plants) in the warm water.
The noise of all the birds was amazing. Every now and then, a few flamingos would take off. Their large black-edged wings flapped and their legs were stretched out behind.

I wanted to stay longer, but we had to get back as we are cooking tonight.

African Recipe for Irio

You will need
a saucepan · a spoon

Ingredients

100 g (1 cup) fresh or frozen corn

100 g (1 cup) shelled green peas

6 medium potatoes, peeled
and chopped

3 tbsp butter
a pinch of salt and pepper

What to do:

1

Boil the potatoes in a saucepan of water until soft.

2

Add the corn and peas. Simmer until soft. Add more water if needed.

3

Drain the water and mash the mixture with a spoon.

4

Mix in the salt, pepper and butter. Serve hot.

Day 4

7.00 a.m. Breakfast

8.00 a.m. Waterhole watching

African
elephant

1.00 p.m. Lunch

4.00 p.m. Rhino sanctuary

7.30 p.m. Dinner

I began the day by watching the waterhole in front of our camp.

The herd of elephants had arrived early for their first drink of the day. There were eight adults and two younger ones. The babies were fun to watch as they played in the water.

After bathing, the elephants sucked up dust into their trunks. They then sprayed the dust all over their bodies. Our guide told us that the dust acts as an insect repellent. It also stops the sun from damaging their skin. We watched as the elephants ate grasses. They tore up the grasses with their trunks. They would loosen some plants by kicking the roots with their front foot. They shook the dust off the roots before popping them into their mouths.

It is hard to imagine why these amazing giants are in danger from people.

What is a group of elephants called?

Save the Elephants

Why are African elephants important?

Elephants create clearings in forests, which allow new trees to grow. They stop bushes growing big in the savannah. This makes areas of lower grasses for the browsing and grazing animals.

Watch me.

Quick links

▷ Safaris
▷ Africa
▷ Baby elephants
▷ Videos
▷ More articles

The aims of elephant conservation:

- ℮ to improve laws to stop poaching.
- ℮ to work with farmers and villages to value elephants.
- ℮ to stop elephants raiding crops, using non-harming methods.

Why do elephants need help?

The population of African elephants has halved due to poaching. Poachers have killed them for their ivory trunks and, in some cases, for meat. Elephants have a large range as they move about to find food. Their routes were once forests or savannah, but now roads, farmland and villages are on the routes. This causes conflict with people.

This afternoon, I came face-to-face with another of the Big Five – the rhinos. They were magnificent. One of the black rhinos we saw had its horn removed. This would protect it from poachers. The number of rhinos was once very low in East Africa. However, a group of rhinos was brought to live in this large protected area.

Just before we left, we met Baraka, a blind black rhino. He is looked after by the rangers. Rhinos do not have very good eyesight, but a blind one would not survive in the wild.

Why would a blind rhino not survive in the wild?

Dear Mum and Dad,
We went up in a helicopter today to search for one of the white rhinos. The trackers aim to see each of the rhinos at least once every five days. It was an amazing ride. You can see so much from the air. We flew over a herd of galloping zebras. Their black-and-white stripes were a blur. To our relief, we spotted the rhino and he was looking well. Time is flying by. Only one more day before we fly home!
See you soon, Katie x

Mr and Mrs Collins
56, Canning Drive,
Westport,
Sussex,
United Kingdom
WE5 6UT

Day 5

7.30 a.m. Breakfast

9.00 a.m. Visit local village

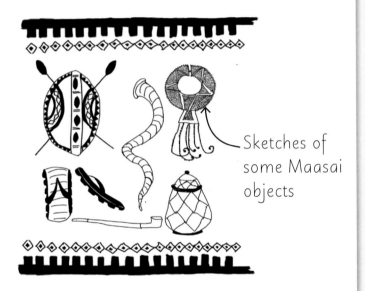

Sketches of some Maasai objects

1.00 p.m. Lunch

Afternoon free to rest and pack

6.00 p.m. Dinner

7.30 p.m. Night game drive

Our visit to a Maasai family began with the welcome jumping dance.

The tall Maasai warriors performed the dance. Their bodies were covered in red ochre (earth) and they jumped very high.

Around their homes, there is a circular fence known as the kraal. It is made from acacia thorns. The thorns prevent lions from entering to attack the cattle, goats and sheep.

This necklace was
huge and colourful.

The cows are very important to the Maasai. They provide food, milk to drink and are sold for money. The boys take them out to find grazing areas every day.

The women were dressed in bright, coloured clothes and wore large, beaded necklaces. The beads were mainly red (the colour of the Maasai), blue (the colour of the sky) and green (the colour of the grass). One woman showed us how they made their loaf-shaped homes. She used mud, sticks, grass, cow dung and cow's urine.

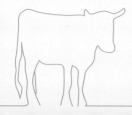

Maasai Village

The Maasai are a group of people, or tribe, who live in Kenya and Tanzania. They have kept many of their old traditions.

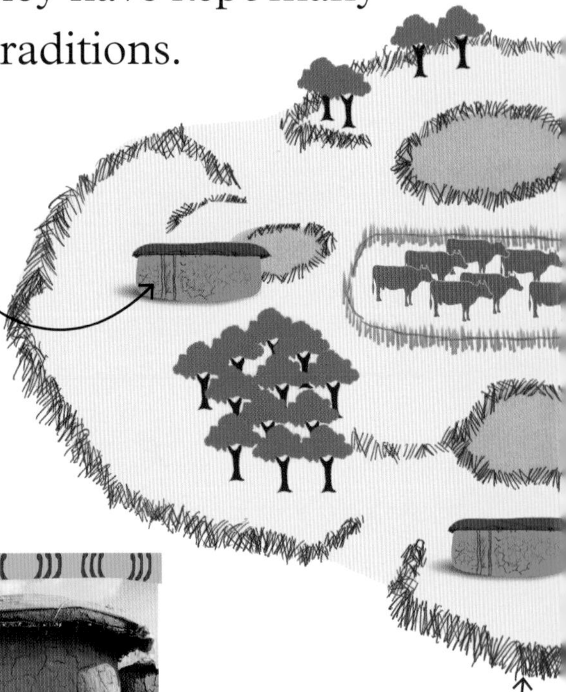

Loaf-shaped or round huts

The kraal (thorny fence)

The Maasai live in huts in a small village called an enkang.

It is dark and smoky inside the huts. The Maasai prepare meals on the fire. They mainly sleep on animal skins on the floor. They store fuel and keep small animals in the hut.

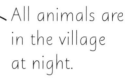

All animals are in the village at night.

Gaps in the fence are blocked at night.

A woman adding mud to the roof of her hut.

This evening's night drive was a wonderful end to our trip. The highlight was seeing the last of the Big Five – a leopard. In the glare of the spotlight, we watched it prowling through the bush. It was on its nightly hunt. Its glowing eyes stared straight at me.

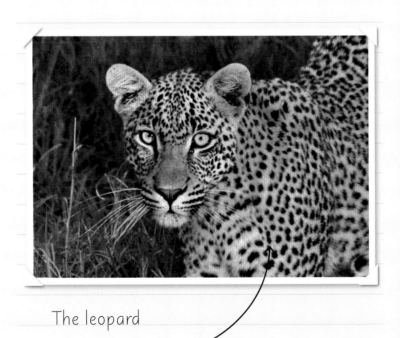

The leopard watched us, too.

Animals behave differently at night. Hippos were out of the water, grazing on the riverbanks. We saw animals that would be asleep in their burrows during the day. The savannah was eerie but magical.

How would you feel if you were out in the savannah at night-time?

Night-time Animals File

Bat-eared fox
Its large ears help to cool down and hear well.

Porcupine
Its sharp spines, or quills, give protection.

Aardvark
Its very long tongue licks up lots of termites.

Bushbabies
Its big eyes help to see very well in the dark.

Mongoose
Its light body helps it to escape from danger.

Honey badger
It is brave and fearless. Few animals will fight it.

African civet
Its sharp claws help to move easily in trees.

59

Safari Quiz

1. Which antelope has black stripes on its face and sides?

2. What is a group of hippos called?

3. Can you name the Big Five?

4. How far away can a male lion's roar be heard?

5. Which night-time animal has a long tongue?

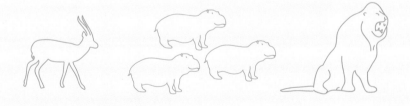

Answers on page 64.

Glossary

migrating
moving from one
area to another

monitor
watch and
check over
a period of time

myth
legend, fable or
traditional story

poaching
killing and stealing
animals without
permission

research
study of materials
and observations
to find out facts

savannah
large area of
flat grassland with
a few trees found
in hot countries

tribesman
member of
the traditional
hunting people

venomous
able to pass on
venom (poison)
in a bite or a sting

waterhole
hollow filled with
water, forming a pool,
that is used by
animals as a bathing
and drinking place

Guide for Parents

DK Reads is a three-level interactive reading adventure series for children, developing the habit of reading widely for both pleasure and information. These chapter books have an exciting main narrative interspersed with a range of reading genres to suit your child's reading ability, as required by the National Curriculum. Each book is designed to develop your child's reading skills, fluency, grammar awareness, and comprehension in order to build confidence and engagement when reading.

Ready for a *Starting to Read Alone* book

YOUR CHILD SHOULD

- be able to read most words without needing to stop and break them down into sound parts.
- read smoothly, in phrases and with expression. By this level, your child will be mostly reading silently.
- self-correct when some word or sentence doesn't sound right.

A VALUABLE AND SHARED READING EXPERIENCE

For some children, text reading, particularly non-fiction, requires much effort but adult participation can make this both fun and easier. So here are a few tips on how to use this book with your child.

TIP 1 Check out the contents together before your child begins:

- invite your child to check the blurb, contents page and layout of the book and comment on it.
- ask your child to make predictions about the story.
- chat about the information your child might want to find out.

TIP 2 Encourage fluent and flexible reading:

- support your child to read in fluent, expressive phrases, making full use of punctuation and thinking about the meaning.

- encourage your child to slow down and check information where appropriate.

TIP 3 Indicators that your child is reading for meaning:

- your child will be responding to the text if he/she is self-correcting and varying his/her voice.
- your child will want to chat about what he/she is reading or is eager to turn the page to find out what will happen next.

TIP 4 Praise, share and chat:

- the factual pages tend to be more difficult than the story pages, and are designed to be shared with your child.
- encourage your child to recall specific details after each chapter.
- provide opportunities for your child to pick out interesting words and discuss what they mean.
- discuss how the author captures the reader's interest, or how effective the non-fiction layouts are.
- ask questions about the text. These help to develop comprehension skills and awareness of the language used.

A FEW ADDITIONAL TIPS

- Read to your child regularly to demonstrate fluency, phrasing and expression; to find out or check information; and for sharing enjoyment.
- Encourage your child to reread favourite texts to increase reading confidence and fluency.
- Check that your child is reading a range of different types, such as poems, jokes and following instructions.

Series consultant **Shirley Bickler** is a longtime advocate of carefully crafted, enthralling texts for young readers. Her LIFT initiative for infant teaching was the model for the National Literacy Strategy Literacy Hour, and she is co-author of *Book Bands for Guided Reading* published by Reading Recovery based at the Institute of Education.

Index

Answers to the Safari Quiz:

1. Thomson's gazelle; 2. A pod; 3. Lion, African elephant, Cape buffalo, leopard and rhinoceros; 4. 8 km (5 mi); 5. Aardvark.